FRIENDS
OF ACPL

Rocky's workshop

SILVERSTONE

IVINGHOE HILL

The scrapyard

Mr. Oldcastle's cottage

GUMDROP

FOLLETT PUBLISHING COMPANY
CHICAGO

GUMDROP
on the Move

Written and Illustrated by
VAL BIRO

Copyright © 1969 by Val Biro. First published 1969 by
Brockhampton Press, Ltd., Leicester.

Published 1970 in the United States of America by Follett Publishing Company. All rights reserved.
No part of this book may be reproduced in any form without written permission from the publisher.
Manufactured in the United States of America.

ISBN 0-695-40125-4 Titan binding
ISBN 0-695-80125-2 Trade binding

Library of Congress Catalog Card Number: 79-118925

First Printing
G

Mr. Josiah Oldcastle was
very fond of old cars. He had
a small brown car, a 1934
baby Austin Seven which
he called Araminta. It lived
in a garage with a green door.
Mr. Oldcastle was proud of
his little car and he polished
it every day.
There was another garage there,
with a red door. But it was empty.
"In there," he said to his grandson Robert,
"I had another car once. It was blue, with a black top
and a brass horn: a genuine vintage car of 1926. I had to
sell it years ago. I wonder where it is now."

Just then the mail arrived. There, among the letters and bills, was a catalog for "The Sale by Auction of Veteran and Vintage Vehicles," and there, on the first page, was a picture.

Mr. Oldcastle became very excited. "Look!" he said. "Here it is!! This is surely the very car that I had all those years ago, that lived behind the red door!!! It must be GUMDROP!!!!"

TO BE AUCTIONED

An Austin Clifton Heavy Twelve-Four, vintage 1926, 1660-c.c. four-cylinder side-valve engine, four-speed gearbox, four-wheel brakes. In blue and black livery, black canvas top, brass radiator, lamps, and horn. Complete with battery, spare gas tin, spare wheel. All in excellent condition. Best offer secures.

And it was. When Mr. Oldcastle went to the auction sale the next day, there, sure enough, among the many fine cars and carriages for sale, was Gumdrop. Many people wanted to buy it.

Mr. O'Hara wanted Gumdrop because he was a collector of vintage cars;

Mr. Banger wanted Gumdrop because he was a car dealer, and Mr. Oldcastle wanted Gumdrop because he once owned it himself. "But I only hope it won't be too expensive," he said.

The auction began. People called out a price, others called
out a higher one, and the highest bidder secured the car.
Many were sold this way until it was Gumdrop's turn.
"What am I bid for this remarkable vehicle?" shouted
the auctioneer. People bid briskly for Gumdrop,
and the price got higher, higher, and higher.
At last the auctioneer cried,
"Going, Going, Gone!"
and banged his hammer.
"Sold to Mr. Banger!"

Mr. O'Hara did not buy it after all because Gumdrop
wasn't rare enough for him. "And I couldn't buy it after
all," said Mr. Oldcastle sadly to Robert when he got home,
"because Gumdrop wasn't cheap enough for me."

So Mr. Banger drove Gumdrop to his showrooms. He polished the car until it shone, and then he put it among all the new cars in his window. "This old-timer should help to sell my modern cars," he said.

Many people
stopped to admire Gumdrop,
but only a few of them bought
new cars. Mr. Banger was disappointed.

Archibald Gridline came
into the shop one day. "I don't
want a new car," he said, "but will
you sell me that blue vintage Austin there?
I want to race it at Silverstone."
"I might as well," said Mr. Banger, "because after all
the car isn't smart enough for me."

So Archibald Gridline drove
Gumdrop to his garage.
There he removed the top
so that Gumdrop could go
faster, and he unscrewed the
horn and put it into the toolbox.
Next day he drove Gumdrop to Silverstone and entered
in the All-Comers Vintage Sports Car Five-Lap Handicap Race.

The vintage cars were roaring around the circuit. Gumdrop went faster and faster, but the other cars went faster and faster still. Suddenly there was a big clatter in the engine. Gumdrop stopped.

"That's the big end!" cried Gridline. "I'm out of the race!" He was very disappointed.

Rocky Basher came to help push Gumdrop off the course. "I'll buy that car off you," he said. "I want to race it at the Autocross."

"You can have it," said Gridline, "because after all the car isn't fast enough for me."

So Rocky Basher drove Gumdrop to his workshop. There he repaired the big end, removed the fenders and lamps to make Gumdrop lighter, and painted the car yellow with green stripes.

Next day he drove Gumdrop to Chartridge and entered in the Autocross Trophy Race. All the other cars were modern, small, and light, and they raced each other around the rough grass track. When Rocky's turn came, Gumdrop slithered and skidded and skipped around the wet grass as fast as possible, but the other cars slithered and skidded around faster still.

Suddenly Gumdrop lurched
forward, spun around, and stopped.
"My wheel has come off!"
cried Rocky. "I'm out of the race!"
He was very disappointed.

Bodger Prescott came to help with the wheel. "Will you
sell me your car?" he asked. "I want to race it at the
Ivinghoe hill-climb." "I will," said Rocky Basher,
"because after all the car isn't light enough for me."

So Bodger Prescott drove
Gumdrop to his shed. There
he removed the windscreen,
the running boards, and the
spare wheel. He then greased
and oiled Gumdrop ready
for next day's big hill-climbing
race for Veteran and
Vintage cars.
The other cars were dashing
up the hill with roaring
engines and crunching
gears. Gumdrop went
as fast as possible,
but the hill was steep
and very slippery.

Gumdrop's engine was roaring too, until there was a
jet of steam coming out of the radiator,
and Gumdrop had to stop. "I'm boiling!"
cried Bodger, "and we're out of
the race!" He was
very disappointed.

Farmer Golightly came
to help, with a can of water.
"That's a useful car you've
got there," he said to Bodger.
"It would help me on the farm."
"You can have it," said Bodger Prescott,
"because after all the car isn't strong enough for me."

So Mr. Golightly drove Gumdrop to his farm. There he removed the number-plates, the doors, and the back seat so that there would be more room for the sacks of corn and bales of straw which he wanted Gumdrop to carry for him. Even so, there wasn't enough room for such big loads. Mr. Golightly was very disappointed. "I'll just have to leave it in the yard," he said, "because after all the car isn't big enough for me."

Gumdrop stayed in the farmyard. Without a top and
a horn, without lamps and fenders, windscreen or running
boards, with no spare wheel, number-plates, back seat, or
doors, and painted yellow with green stripes, Gumdrop
was a strange and sorry sight.

One day, some weeks later,
Mick Mulligan came by.
"That's a funny old car,"
he thought, "but it might fetch
a pound or two at the scrapyard." There was nobody
around, so he quickly jumped into Gumdrop, started the
engine, and drove out of the yard.

Mick Mulligan drove badly
and too fast. Gumdrop
lurched from side to side
and skidded around the corners.
Suddenly, at the sharpest bend
of all, they stopped. They
had to. They had bumped
into a small brown car that
was standing by the roadside.

It was Araminta, Mr. Oldcastle's baby Austin Seven of 1934. Mr. Oldcastle was there himself, trying to mend a puncture, and he was very angry. "Look where you're going, you unmitigated blundering nincompoop!" he shouted at Mick Mulligan. "You've bent my bumper and nearly had me over too!"

Mick was frightened. "I'm sorry, sir," he stammered, "but I can't pay for the damage I've done to your car. Tell you what," he added, "you can have this old heap instead!" Without waiting for a reply, he jumped over the fence and ran away. After all, Gumdrop wasn't nearly valuable enough for him.

Mr. Oldcastle looked at Gumdrop, but did not recognize it. "Odd-looking machine," he said, "though it is an Austin Heavy Twelve-Four right enough, and I could restore it. It would be grand to have another vintage Austin again." And so he hitched Gumdrop to Araminta and they drove home, with Robert steering Gumdrop.

Next day Mr. Oldcastle and Robert drove to the scrapyard in search of the missing parts for Gumdrop. Old
cars and bits and pieces were heaped up everywhere.

"Funny you should ask me,"
said Mr. Ebenezer Hearn, the scrap-
merchant. "Quite a lot of Austin
Twelve-Four parts have come in
lately; only the other day I had
some doors and a seat from
Farmer Golightly! There they
are, with the other bits and
pieces I've had. You can
have the lot, sir!"

Mr. Oldcastle and Robert piled
all the things on top of Araminta's roof,
tied them down securely, and drove home.

The restoration began.
They bolted back the fenders and
running boards, and replaced
the windscreen.

They screwed on the lamps
and hinged up the doors.

They clamped on the top
and put in the back seat.

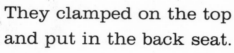

And they screwed the
spare wheel in place again.

Finally, they painted the body blue and the fenders black.
After a week's hard work, the car looked as good as new.

"It looks exactly like my old car now," said Mr. Oldcastle,
"though I wish that this car was actually Gumdrop itself!"
Just then Robert was rummaging in the toolbox while
Mr. Oldcastle polished the engine. "I wonder," he
thought, "if after all . . ." He looked at the engine
number. C.4478. "The same!!" he shouted. "The same
number!!! This must actually be . . ."
"It IS! It IS!" shouted Robert in turn, as he pulled
out the shiny brass horn.
"This is our own original
Gumdrop after all!!"

So Mr. Oldcastle got Gumdrop back again.
They drove proudly to the town the
next week to take part in the
Vintage Car Display.

Farmer Golightly was there,
and he gave Mr. Oldcastle Gumdrop's original
number-plates which he had taken off back at the farm.
The Mayor was there, and he gave Mr. Oldcastle a silver
cup for "The Best Restoration of a Vintage Car."

And there, too, were all the people who had owned
Gumdrop since the Vintage Auction Sale. They came up
to admire Gumdrop and to congratulate Mr. Oldcastle.

There was Mr. O'Hara,
for whom Gumdrop
wasn't rare enough.

There was Mr. Banger,
for whom Gumdrop
wasn't smart enough.

There was Archibald Gridline,
for whom Gumdrop
wasn't fast enough.

There was Rocky Basher,
for whom Gumdrop
wasn't light enough.

There was Bodger Prescott,
for whom Gumdrop
wasn't strong enough.

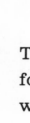

There was Farmer Golightly,
for whom Gumdrop
wasn't big enough.

There was Mick Mulligan even,
for whom Gumdrop
wasn't valuable enough.

And finally, there was Mr. Josiah Oldcastle, who got his
old car back and would keep it forever. For him
Gumdrop was certainly more than good enough.